Sun Mother Wakes the World

AN AUSTRALIAN CREATION STORY

adapted by Diane Wolkstein

pictures by Bronwyn Bancroft

HarperCollinsPublishers

For Ann Cecil Sterman,

whose presence brings healing and delight

—D.W.

For my two mothers, Dorothy and Euphemia

—B.B.

Sun Mother Wakes the World
Text copyright © 2004 by Diane Wolkstein
Illustrations copyright © 2004 by Bronwyn Bancroft
Manufactured in China by South China Printing Company Ltd. All rights reserved.
www.harperchildrens.com

Library of Congress Cataloging-in-Publication Data
Wolkstein, Diane.
Sun Mother wakes the world : an Australian creation story / adapted by Diane Wolkstein ;
pictures by Bronwyn Bancroft.
p.   cm.
Summary: An Aboriginal creation story in which the Sun slowly brings life to the Earth.
ISBN 0-688-13915-9 — ISBN 0-688-13916-7 (lib. bdg.)
[1. Creation—Folklore. 2. Australian aborigines—Folklore. 3. Folklore—Australia.]
I. Bancroft, Bronwyn, ill. II. Title.   PZ8.1.W84 Su 2004   398.2'089'9915—dc21   [E]
2001016932
Designed by Stephanie Bart-Horvath
2 3 4 5 6 7 8 9 10
❖
First Edition

THE INDIGENOUS PEOPLE OF AUSTRALIA believe that their first ancestors created the world and its laws. They also believe that the world is still being created, and they call this continual process of creation The Dreamtime. In order to enter into creation—past, present, and future—the people perform ceremonies during which they describe The Dreamtime in paintings, dances, songs, and stories.

Just as each of their ancestors appeared on earth in a certain place, which is called their Dreaming, so too the place where each person is born is called his or her Dreaming. The birthplaces of the ancestors and the people living on earth are considered sacred. Some people go on journeys (walkabouts) to look after their own birthplaces and the birthplaces of their ancestors. On such occasions, they perform ceremonies to renew themselves and to keep the earth alive.

DARKNESS.

Silence.

No fish swam.

No animal stirred.

The wind did not whisper.

The earth was asleep.

In the sky, Sun Mother was also asleep. Then a soft voice whispered to her, "Wake, wake, my child."

When Sun Mother opened her eyes, light appeared.

"My daughter," the voice spoke again. "It is time for you to wake the sleeping earth." Sun Mother smiled, and the light became brighter.

Swift as a falling star, Sun Mother sped to the earth. The earth was gray and empty. There was no color. No sound. No movement.

Sun Mother began to travel. With each step she took, grass, plants, and trees sprouted in her footprints.

Sun Mother traveled north, south, east, and west, waking all the earth. Then she rested, surrounded by green plants and trees.

Again the voice called to her, "My daughter, it is time for you to go to the dark caves and wake the sleeping animal spirits."

As Sun Mother entered the first dark cave, it was flooded with light. Witchetty grubs, beetles, and caterpillars cried, "*Kkkkt!* Why do you wake us?"

But when the crawling creatures opened their eyes and saw the beauty of Sun Mother, they followed her out of the cave. Insects of every color and shape appeared, and the earth became more beautiful.

As Sun Mother entered the next cave, ice melted under her feet, forming a stream. Her warmth woke the lizards, frogs, and snakes.

"*Ssssssst!* Go away!" they hissed.

But when they opened their eyes and saw beautiful Sun Mother, a stream filled with lizards, frogs, snakes, and fish flowed after her.

Sun Mother then walked to the coldest, darkest cave, accompanied by the crawling, moving creatures. Down, down they went. Along the ledges of the cave were sleeping birds and animals of every kind.

Sun Mother entered the cave. *"HOO-HOOOoooo!"* The cave owl woke first. Soon, the other birds and animals woke, and when they saw the beautiful Sun Mother, they followed her out of the cave.

Sun Mother lay down and rested under a river-gum tree. All the creatures gathered around her, content with the gift of life they had been given. The wind stirred the leaves. The blossoms offered their fragrance. The crickets hummed. After resting, Sun Mother said, "My children, I woke you as a seed is woken in the spring. Now that you are awake, I can return to my home in the sky."

Sun Mother soared up into the western sky. Where was she going?

"Sun Mother, come back!" the animals called fearfully. "Come back!"

The earth became darker and darker. After a time, it was completely dark. The wind did not whisper. No animal stirred. No fish swam. Everything was still.

Then, a little frog croaked. From the corner of her eye, the frog saw Sun Mother returning in the eastern sky.

"Welcome, welcome, Sun Mother!" the animals cried joyously. But Sun Mother did not return to the earth. She glided slowly across the sky to the west.

Again, there was darkness. Yet, this time the animals were not as frightened as they were before. They understood that Sun Mother had returned to her home in the sky and that each day she would visit them on earth.

As time passed, the animals forgot the joy they had felt when they first received the gift of life. They looked at each other, and they wanted what they did not have. They quarreled with one another, and their loud cries reached the home of Sun Mother.

Swift as a falling star, Sun Mother sped to the earth. She gathered everyone together and said, "My children, I love each of you. I wish you to be happy. If you are unhappy with your shape, you will have a chance to change. Consider very carefully what you choose, for the form you choose will be yours for a long time."

Slowly the animals began to change. Wombat chose to have strong claws so he could dig tunnels under the earth. Kangaroo chose to have a pouch so she could keep her babies close to her. Emu chose to have long legs so he could run faster than any other bird. Platypus could not decide what she wanted. So she chose everything. A beak, fur, webbed feet, *and* a tail!

After all the animals were happy with their new forms, Sun Mother wanted to create something new. That night she gave birth to a daughter and a son, Moon and Morning Star.

The next morning Sun Mother called all the creatures together and said, "My children, now when I leave you in the evening, my daughter Moon and my son Morning Star will be with you to give you light."

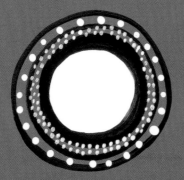

Moon and Morning Star grew brighter. In time, they gave birth to twins, to the first woman and the first man.

"Welcome, welcome!" Sun Mother said to the first woman and the first man. "All around you are your relations—the grass, the hills, the water, the wind, and the animals. This is their place. Now it is yours too. Wherever you go, always return to look after your birthplace.

"Care for the land for the sake of your grandparents as well as for your children and grandchildren. I traveled every step of the earth and it is now alive. Just as I will visit the earth each morning, so you too must walk the land to keep it alive."

With these words, Sun Mother soared up into the sky.

Each morning Sun Mother continues to keep her promise,

bringing light to the earth.

AUTHOR'S NOTE

IN *MYTHS AND LEGENDS* of the Australian Aboriginals, Ramsay Smith attributed the story of Sun Mother to Kardin-Nilla (Laughing Waters), a Karraru woman of the West Coast of South Australia. "Karraru" is a moiety name. Moiety, a way of determining relationship, is inherited from the mother. It can refer to people from different language groups and regions. So Kardin-Nilla may have been a Wirangu person, the group who were the original people of the Streaky Bay region, for example. She may equally have been a Mirning person, or even a Kokatha person from the Gawler Ranges region. The Dieri language group also used the Karraru moiety.

Although Ramsay Smith copyrighted and published *Myths and Legends of the Australian Aboriginals* as his own work, he did not collect the stories firsthand. Most of them were gathered and written down by David Unaipon, a Nigarrindjeri man from the lower Murray River region. Many of Unaipon's legends contain a mix of Aboriginal and European themes, and he may have made significant changes to the Sun Mother story Kardin-Nilla told him.

I made three journeys to Australia to find out about the story of Sun Mother. On the third journey, Bill Edwards, a lecturer in Aboriginal studies at the University of South Australia, was able to confirm this information. It has also been verified by Melissa Clancy, information officer at the Indigenous Information Centre of the South Australian Museum, and by Dr. Phillip Jones, an anthropologist from the South Australian Museum. I am most grateful for their help.

My thanks also to folklorist Dick Kimber, botanist Peter Latz, painter Pansy Napangardi, potter Thancoupi, and bush guide Peter Yates.

Both the artist and I have made every effort to locate the people descended from those who originally told the story *Sun Mother Wakes the World* is based upon. If any are alive, no disrespect is intended, and we are eager to credit them in future editions.